The Mystery of the Tree Rings

The Mystery of the Tree Rings

by MARK MEIERHENRY and DAVID VOLK

Illustrated by JASON FOLKERTS

SOUTH DAKOTA STATE HISTORICAL SOCIETY PRESS   PIERRE

This publication was funded, in part, by the
Great Plains Education Foundation, Inc., Aberdeen, S.Dak.

Library of Congress Cataloging-in-Publication Data
Meierhenry, Mark V.
The mystery of the tree rings / by Mark Meierhenry and David Volk ;
illustrated by Jason Folkerts.
p. cm.
ISBN 978-0-9798940-0-8
1. Tree-rings—Juvenile literature. I. Volk, David, 1947–
II. Folkerts, Jason, ill. III. Title.
QK477.2.A6M45 2008
582.16—dc22
2008019787

Printed in Korea

12 11 10 09 08   1 2 3 4 5

This book is dedicated to men and women foresters across the nation and to people everywhere who plant and protect trees.

The Mystery of the Tree Rings

A long time ago . . .

Deep in the Black Hills of what is now South Dakota, a tall tree rose into the sky. It was a ponderosa pine. Pinecones hung from its branches. One day, a pinecone tumbled down to the forest floor.

The cone contained fifty seeds. Birds, mice, and chipmunks ate many of them. Cold winds and snow froze many more, but one seed fell into a sheltered spot and began to grow.

That single seedling grew for the next seven hundred years. It was growing before Columbus set sail for the New World. It welcomed the arrival of the Lakota Indians into the Black Hills. It watched as Lewis and Clark went west on the Journey of Discovery.

Many years later, the old tree looked down and saw a small, scared boy sitting under its branches.

The mystery of the tree rings was about to be revealed.

Max and Hannah jumped out of their bunk beds at their grandparent's farm. They dressed quickly and raced downstairs. Grandpa had promised them an adventure, and they were eager to get started.

Their mad dash took them through the kitchen where Grandma grabbed and hugged them.

"You two be quiet for awhile. Grandpa is writing in his journal," she said as she took cinnamon rolls from the oven.

The twins laughed when their stomachs both grumbled at the same time. They sat down to eat.

"What does Grandpa write in his journal?" Hannah asked as she started to eat a homemade roll.

"Oh, he writes down a little bit of everything. What we are doing, what the weather is like, how big you kids are getting. He puts down events, big and small. He calls it his 'window to the past.' In the years to come, he will be able to recall special days like today," Grandma replied.

"If you two are finished eating all your grandmother's cinnamon rolls," Grandpa said from the doorway, "let's get going on our adventure.

"Before we go, get your measuring sticks. I want to record how much you've grown."

"Where are we going?" Max asked as they crawled into their grandfather's pickup truck.

"We're headed to the Black Hills," he said.

Max and Hannah cheered. They loved to travel over the rolling hills that ran westward from Grandpa's farm. Some of the roads went up and down as sharply as the roller coaster they rode at the carnival.

From the windows, they could see wild animals running free on the prairie. A herd of antelope grazed on a bluff. A whole flock of wild turkeys stood near the road.

Hannah was surprised to see how tall and skinny the wild turkeys were compared to their fat cousins on the farm. She watched a coyote loping across a field. She hoped the coyote did not make an early Thanksgiving feast of the turkeys.

"Grandpa, how long have you kept your journal?" Max suddenly asked.

"A long time. I started it when I was a little older than you are."

The twins looked at each other in surprise.

"Whoa," said Max, "that *is* a long time."

"Yes, it is, Max, but today we are going to visit something that has been keeping a journal for over seven hundred years."

"No way!" Max said. "No way can a journal be kept that long!"

"You'll see," Grandpa said, smiling.

After a few hours, they drove into the Black Hills. The winding roads and mountains covered with pine and aspen trees were different from the rolling prairie they had just crossed.

Grandpa pulled the pickup into a parking lot. The twins jumped out, ready to explore the trail leading up the mountain.

Grandpa led the way into the trees.

"Come on, you two, keep up. That journal has been waiting long enough," he called back.

Max and Hannah thought that Grandpa was joking, but they were ready to play along.

Max lagged behind as they climbed the trail. He spotted what he thought was a seashell. It was imbedded in a rock just off the trail. He went to investigate. It *was* a shell, and he could see other fossils in the stones. How could there be seashells in the mountains, he wondered. Little did he know that millions of years ago the Black Hills were covered by an ocean.

He turned to ask Grandpa about the fossils.

Max's heart sank. Where were Grandpa and Hannah? He did not see them anywhere. He could no longer hear their voices. He was so turned around in the trees and rocks he did not even know the way back to the trail.

He yelled, but the tall trees swallowed up the sound of his voice. He ran among the trees until he remembered what Grandpa had always said: "Stay put if you are ever lost." Grandpa would come back. Max knew he would.

Tired and thirsty, Max sat down under a large tree and leaned his head against the trunk. All around, the trees looked gigantic. They blocked the light from the forest floor—it was dark and scary.

"Hello, little boy," said a gentle voice, rustling through the tree branches. "Are you okay?"

Max looked around. The tree seemed to be talking to him.

"Yes . . . I mean, no, I am not okay. I am lost and scared and now I think I have a tree talking to me," Max replied faintly.

The tree chuckled. "You are fine. My name is Ponderosa, but my friends call me Rosa. What's your name?"

"My name is Max, and my friends call me . . . uh . . . Max. You haven't seen an old guy and a girl about my age, have you?"

"No, but I have seen and thought about a good many things in the 760 some years I have stood here," Rosa said.

"760 years! Have you really been around that long?" Max asked.

"Not only have I been here that long, I've kept a journal of all those years," the tree said. "It tells what happened to me and what happened to the land during that time."

Max looked up at Rosa skeptically. That was the second time he had heard about a journal more than seven hundred years old.

"Where is your journal?" Max asked in disbelief.

"It's inside me. Look over there," Rosa said. "That tree stump was my uncle. Soldiers of the Seventh Calvary cut him down when George Armstrong Custer came through here in 1874.

"I always wondered what happened to Custer," she mumbled to herself. "He never came back.

"Anyway, do you see those rings on my uncle's trunk?" she asked Max.

Max looked down at the stump. The rings circled one inside the other all the way to the center of the trunk.

"The rings tell the story," Rosa said. "Each year we trees add a ring of growth outside of the one from the year before. The rings keep track of our age and tell the story of this land and its weather. Thick rings mean lots of sun and rain. Trees grow fat in such years. Thin rings mean hard times and little rain.

"To read my uncle's journal, you start in the center and work outward. A bunch of thin rings together mean that there were years of drought or a cycle of cold weather. Some rings tell of insect attacks, and forest fires are also part of the record.

"Max, you won't believe it, but I was struck by lighting once, and that, too, is recorded within my trunk. All told by my rings," Rosa said wisely.

"I was here before the Pilgrims landed at Jamestown," she boasted. "I was here before the United States was united. I saw the Lakota Indians set up their first tepees in these hills. I even watched a man carve four faces on a mountain called Rushmore.

"Remembering the past can help us understand the present and plan for our future," she added.

Max started to ask Rosa a question, but his whole body suddenly shivered. He realized it was growing dark and cold.

"Enough about my journal and rings," Rosa whispered. "Why don't you lean back against my trunk?"

Rosa began to sway gently. Max listened to the wind rush through her branches and felt safe again.

"Max! Max! Where have you been?" his sister shouted, shaking him anxiously.

Max opened his eyes and saw Hannah. Grandpa was trying to look angry, but Max could see that he was far too happy about finding Max to be mad at him.

"You got yourself lost at the very spot we were heading for," Grandpa said after hugging and scolding him. "If you are through scaring me, I'll tell you about this ancient tree. It has been keeping a journal for over 760 years."

Grandpa started telling about the journals that trees keep within their trunks. Max smiled. His friend Rosa had already told him, but it was a good story, and he wanted to hear it again.

With one last look at the old tree, Grandpa and the twins headed out of the forest. It was time to start their trip back to the farm.

"See that little tree over there?" Grandpa asked, pointing to a pine about as tall as Max or Hannah.

"If we could see its rings, I bet we would discover that it is about the same age as the two of you," Grandpa said. "Let's hope it grows for another seven hundred years or more."

Max looked back and saw Rosa standing proudly on the hill behind them. He waved to her, and while he could not be sure, he thought he saw her branches waving goodbye in return.

"Grandpa, our measuring sticks are just like tree rings. Each mark tells how much we grew," Hannah said the next morning back at the farm. She was studying the measurements they had made on their sticks.

"Right, Hannah," Grandpa said. "Like a tree's rings, the marks on your stick record your personal growth. Today, I'm giving you your first journals, too, so that you can record other things. Write down all that you saw and did yesterday in the Black Hills. It will help you remember our adventures."

"Hmmmm, do you suppose I'll see as many things as Rosa did?" Max asked as he started to write.

"Who?" Grandpa and Hannah asked.

Max smiled.

"It's a secret," he whispered to himself.

Meet the real Rosa. She is a ponderosa pine growing in the Black Hills of South Dakota. Scientists say that this tree was a seedling in the year 1241 A.D. To find this out, they took a core sample from the trunk and counted the rings.

Start your own journal.

Date: _____

Place: _____

_____

_____

_____

_____

_____

_____

_____

_____

_____

_____

_____

_____